. . . for parents and teachers

I Hate Boys/I Hate Girls is a very special book dealing with a very special stage.

As stages go, hating boys or hating girls may not be a Mount Everest, but it can be a rough little Catskill for everyone concerned — children, parents, and teachers.

As adults, we can help children by reassuring them that their feelings are not unusual or weird. And we can help them recall other stages they've already survived.

Some children hate asparagus until, much later, they discover hollandaise sauce. Sometimes the children who have to be hauled to the bathtub turn out to be the teenagers who take three showers a day. In many families there's a little sister who whines for an entire year, or an older brother who thinks it's perfectly acceptable to practice burping three hours a day.

Happily, these stages pass, and even small children can remember their passings. During any trying stage, we've tried to remind our children of those other normal phases. A child needs calm reassurance that he or she is normal *right now*, and that the feelings about this stage — whether they match or differ from their peer group's feelings — are acceptable.

Most of all, children need reassurance that it's okay to like someone (even a member of the opposite sex) whether or not their other friends approve. Childhood friendships are truly special friendships, and they need encouragement.

PAULA AND DICK McDONALD
AUTHORS OF *LOVING FREE*

Copyright © 1980, Raintree Publishers Inc.

All rights reserved. No part of this book may be
reproduced or utilized in any form or by any means,
electronic or mechanical, including photocopying,
recording, or by any information storage and retrieval
system, without permission in writing from the Publisher.
Inquiries should be addressed to Raintree Childrens Books,
205 West Highland Avenue, Milwaukee, Wisconsin 53203.

Library of Congress Number: 79-24056

    2 3 4 5 6 7 8 9 0 84 83 82

Printed in the United States of America.

Library of Congress Cataloging in Publication Data

Hogan, Paula Z
   I hate boys, I hate girls.

   SUMMARY: Peter and Dawn go from being friends
to being enemies after his male friends make fun
of him for having a "girl friend."
   [1. Friendship — Fiction.   2.   Individuality —
Fiction] I. Hockerman, Dennis. II. Title.
PZ7.H68313Iah   [Fic]   79-24056
ISBN 0-8172-1358-9 lib. bdg.

I HATE
BOYS
I HATE
GIRLS

by Paula Z. Hogan

illustrated by Dennis Hockerman

introduction by Paula and Dick McDonald

♠
RAINTREE CHILDRENS BOOKS
Milwaukee • Toronto • Melbourne • London

"If there isn't somebody my age in that new family next door," I said to myself, "I'm just going to die!"

I was doing a lot of talking to myself that summer. It was the loneliest summer of my life. It seemed as if everyone in my whole neighborhood was either too big or too little to play with me.

I watched the movers move in the new family's things. And I watched the new family drive up in its car.

"No kids," I mumbled to myself.

Just as I turned to go back in my house,
I heard a voice.

"Oh, Frankenstein! It doesn't look like
there's any kids around here."

I looked back at the car. Climbing out
of it was a girl about my size.

"I'm a kid," I said. "And I live
next door."

"Hi!" she said. "My name's Dracula.
But you can call me Dawn. What's yours?"

"Um, King Kong. You can call
me Peter. I like monsters too. . . ."

I had a feeling I wasn't going to have to
talk to myself anymore.

It wasn't long before Dawn and I were
doing stuff together almost every day.

We watched old monster movies on TV.
We had squirt gun fights. We played
catch and traded baseball cards. We had
bicycle races down our street.

When it came time for the first day of school, we even took the bus together.

As we were sitting down, I heard Tony call from somewhere behind us: "Peter's got a girl friend! Peter's got a girl friend!"

A lot of the other kids snickered. Dawn and I didn't look at each other.

At lunchtime, Tony made fun of me again. "Where's your girl friend? When are you getting married?"

"I don't have a girl friend," I said. "I . . . I don't even like girls!"

"Good," said Tony. "Then you can be in our club."

"What club?"

"The I Hate Girls Club. David, Derek, and I belong to it."

"Well, now I belong to it too," I said.

On the way home from school, I sat near Tony and his friends on the bus. I saw Dawn coming down the aisle toward me.

"I'm sure glad I belong to the I Hate Girls Club," I said loudly. "Girls are so dumb!"

Dawn looked at me for a minute, then walked past me. "You're the dummy," I heard her mumble.

The next morning, Dawn sat in the front of the bus with Jean and Gretchen.

"I can't wait till Saturday," Dawn was saying loud enough for everyone on the bus to hear. "Then we can have the first meeting of the I Hate Boys Club. Boys are such monsters!"

On Saturday afternoon, we had a meeting of the I Hate Girls Club in Tony's backyard.

"Let's play a trick on the girls," said Tony.

"What do you want to do?" Derek asked. "Put spiders down their backs?"

"Hide behind a bush and get them with our squirt guns?" asked David.

"That all sounds like fun," Tony said. "But I think I have an even better idea."

Tony told us his plan.

"I love it," said Derek.

"What a riot!" said David.

I didn't say anything. I thought it sounded like a mean thing to do. But I was sort of afraid to say anything. I was afraid they would start teasing me again about having a girl friend.

We hurried over to the playhouse where Dawn and her friends were having their I Hate Boys Club meeting. I tiptoed up to the window.

"Every boy I know is a real rat," I heard Gretchen say.

"Right!" said Dawn. "First they're your friends. The next day they're not."

I gulped. I knew she was right.

Then Tony yelled, "Charge!"

He and the others opened the playhouse window and threw pail after pail of dusty dirt inside. My job was to hold the door shut so the girls couldn't escape.

"Let us out!" the girls shouted.

As we started running back to Tony's house, we could hear the girls coughing and choking.

I didn't stay long at Tony's house. I wanted to be by myself for a while.

After supper that night, my dad said to me, "You look as if you need cheering up. Why don't you go over to Dawn's house?"

"It's against club rules," I said. "No visiting at girls' houses is allowed."

"What are you talking about?"

I explained to him about the I Hate Girls Club. I told him how the boys made fun of me for being friends with Dawn. I didn't mention anything about the kind of tricks we played on girls.

"But I thought you and Dawn were good friends," my dad said.

"We were," I said.

"And that you liked Dawn as a person," he said.

"I did."

"You mean you just lost a good friend because of what other people were saying about you?"

I didn't know what to say. *I guess Dawn was right about my being a dummy,* I thought to myself.

I thought about the I Hate Girls Club and the I Hate Boys Club all night.

By the next morning, I had decided that clubs were silly.

After breakfast, I grabbed my favorite squirt gun and went next door.

"Dawn's in her room, Peter," said Dawn's mother. "Go right up."

I poked my head in Dawn's doorway.

She looked up from her book. "What do you want?" she asked. "If you came over just to throw more dirt at me, I'll—"

"I came to say I'm sorry," I said.

"Then what are you doing with that squirt gun? If you think I need a bath, you're crazy. I've already had three baths since yesterday!"

29

"I . . . I thought maybe we could have a squirt gun fight, or something," I said.

"I don't want to fight," she said, reaching for my squirt gun. "All *I* want to do is squirt *you*!"

Then she started squirting. And the wetter I got, the more we laughed. Soon we forgot all about hating each other.

It was much more fun to be friends.